MARIMBA BOOKS
An imprint of The Hudson Publishing Group LLC
356 Glenwood Avenue, East Orange, New Jersey 07017

Text copyright © 2011 by Margo Sorenson. Illustrations copyright © 2011 by Priscilla Garcia Burris.

Special book excerpts or customized printings can also be created to fit specific needs.
For details, write or phone the office of the Marimba special sales manager:

Marimba Books, 356 Glenwood Avenue, East Orange, New Jersey 07017, 973 672-7701
MARIMBA BOOKS and the Marimba Books logo are trademarks of The Hudson Publishing Group LLC.

ISBN-13: 978-1-160349-027-6   ISBN-10: 1-160349-027-2
10 9 8 7 6 5 4 3 2 1

Printed in Canada

Carol Ann trudged down the path to her new classroom.

"Look at the pink, fluffy flowers, Carol Ann!" Mom said.

Carol Ann scuffed her shoes on the pebbles.

"Feel the warm Hawaiian trade winds blow, Carol Ann!" Mom said.

Carol Ann shoved her hands down inside her jeans pockets.

"Don't the palm trees make a lovely rustling sound?"
Mom asked.

Carol Ann scrunched up her nose.

"Come on, Carol Ann," Mom said.

"You don't want to be late to your new school!"

Thunk! Carol Ann kicked a little stone right at a palm tree.

"You'll make so many new friends," her mother said.

Carol Ann made a face.

Carol Ann didn't want new friends. Nope.

She just wanted her old friends—
Robert, Jasmine, and Emily.

She didn't want fluffy, pink flowers. *YUCK!*

She didn't want warm trade winds. *Nuh-UH.*

She didn't want rustling, palm trees. *Not at ALL.*

And she definitely didn't want a new school.

Carol Ann and her mom stopped in front of a red classroom door.

"Here we are," Mom said.

"What are these?" asked Carol Ann.

Dozens of pairs of shoes were lined up outside the classroom door — rubber flip-flops, sandals, sneakers, and flats.

They all looked about her size.

"I don't have to take off my shoes, too, do I?" Carol Ann asked Mom.

"We'll find out, soon,"
Mom answered.

"Let's go in and meet your
new third-grade teacher,
Ms. Kishimoto."

Carol Ann took a deep breath
and opened the door.

Mom gave her a hug.

"I'll pick you up after school, dear,"
she said.

"Hello! You must be Carol Ann,"
the teacher said with a smile.

As Mom shut the door behind her,
Carol Ann stood there, all alone.

Twenty-six pairs of eyes stared at her.

There were almond-shaped black eyes and brown eyes.

There were round black eyes and big blue eyes.

Carol Ann wanted to shrink so small
that none of the eyes could see her.

"Maile will show you to your seat," said the teacher.

"Your desk is this way, Carol Ann," Maile told her politely.

Maile wore a fluffy pink flower behind one ear.
Carol Ann saw a lot of the other girls wore flowers, too.

Carol Ann followed Maile.

Maile smiled and sat down at the desk next to hers.

Carol Ann put her backpack, her lunch, and her snack under her desk.

"This is Carol Ann, from the Mainland," Ms. Kishimoto announced to the class.

"Let's all wish her *aloha!*"

A chorus of voices answered,

"Aloha, Carol Ann!"

What did that mean? What were they saying?

"Aloha is our word for welcome, goodbye, and love—all in one, Carol Ann," said Ms. Kishimoto.

"It's more special than just 'hello'."

What was wrong with just 'hello' anyway? Carol Ann wondered.

Was she going to have to learn a whole new language, too?

"It's time to get into your reading groups, class.
Teh-Wei, please take Carol Ann with you to the
Mongoose reading group for today," said Ms. Kishimoto.

Kids hurried to their reading groups.
A tall boy with a black buzz cut grinned at Carol Ann
and motioned to her.

She followed him to a circle of kids on chairs.
They smiled at her.

"I'm Kawika," said a boy with brown hair and freckles.

"I'm Sachi," a girl giggled. She had star-shaped white flowers tucked around her black pigtails.

"My name is Rafael," added a boy with black hair.

"And of course, I'm Teh-Wei," Teh-Wei said.
Carol Ann tried out a little smile.

How would she learn all those new names?
She slid down in her chair.

Soon, the reading period ended.

Ms. Kishimoto announced,
"Time for recess, class! Get your snacks."

Recess! Carol Ann's heart sank to the tops
of her shoes. What would she do now?
Who would she play with?

This wasn't anything like her old school and her old friends.

How she wished she were back there right now!

Carol Ann lined up at the door with the other kids.
She kept her head down.

Her heart pounded under her shirt.
Maile squeezed in line next to her.

"Come play with us on the swings,
Carol Ann," invited Maile.

That was what Carol Ann's friend
Jasmine used to say.

"Carol Ann, would you like to try some of the musubi my mother made for snack?" asked Sachi. Her eyes twinkled.

Carol Ann's friend Emily used to share her grandma's cookies.

"We eat our snacks together under the banyan tree, Carol Ann. Come on," Kawika said.

"My auntie made some great mango shortbread."

Carol Ann remembered how her friend Robert always got all the kids together.

"Here, Carol Ann."

Maile held out a fluffy pink flower.
It looked just like the flowers Carol
Ann had seen this morning along
the path.

"Put this hibiscus behind your ear,
like mine," Maile said, with a smile.

Carol Ann felt her face turn warm with happiness.
She tucked the flower behind her ear, just like Maile's.

What if Mom could see her now? Wouldn't she be surprised! Carol Ann blinked. Wait — wouldn't Mom like a flower, too?

"May I please have one for my mother?" Carol Ann asked. "Of course," Maile said.

Maile gave Carol Ann another pink flower.

Carol Ann carefully put the other pink hibiscus in her shirt pocket.

There was something else important, Carol Ann remembered.

Carol Ann asked Maile, "How do you say hello and goodbye and love all at the same time? Ah – aho – ?"

"Oh!" Maile giggled. "You mean 'aloha'!"

"A – lo – ha," Carol Ann repeated slowly.
After school, she would give Mom the flower to wear.

Then she would say, "Aloha!"
And Mom would hug her.

Carol Ann smiled back at Maile.
"Okay," she said. "I'm ready!"

And Carol Ann raced with Maile to the banyan tree to join the rest of her friends.

Margo Sorenson

Born in Washington, DC, **Margo Sorenson** spent the first seven years of her life in Spain and Italy, where books became her earliest friends. She finished school in California, graduating from UCLA. After teaching high school and middle school, Margo began work as a full-time writer and has since published 25 books, including *Danger Marches to the Palace; Queen Luili'uokalani* and *Secret Heroes*. Margo says she loves writing for young readers because they really enjoy "living" the lives of the characters in books. When she isn't writing, she loves visiting her grandchildren, playing golf, reading, watching sports, traveling, and hearing from her readers. After living in Hawaii and Minnesota, Margo and her husband now live in California. Margo's Hawaiian name, Leipua'ala, given to her by a Hawaiian family friend, means "lasting gifts for children."

Priscilla Garcia Burris

Illustrator, designer and author, **Priscilla Garcia Burris** was born and raised in Southern California. An artist from a very early age, she earned degrees in both Fashion Design and Early Childhood Education, and taught pre-school for several years. She serves on the Board of Advisors for the Society of Children's Book Writers and Illustrators, and she has illustrated educational, mass maket and trade books and other materials for children, parents and teachers. Her published books include *Five Green and Speckled Frogs*, which she wrote and illustrated; *What Do Angels Do?*, and *I Love You All Day Long*, which she illustrated.